CHRISTMAS TREASURY

THE GOLDEN
CHRISTMAS TREASURY

25 STORIES, POEMS, AND CAROLS

Compiled and edited by Rick Bunsen

A GOLDEN BOOK · NEW YORK
Western Publishing Company, Inc., Racine, Wisconsin 53404

Illustrators

Anthony Accardo, pages 16–21, 64–70

Tony de Luna, pages 44–46

John O'Brien, pages 31–36, 47–52

Christopher Santoro, pages 26–29

Gloria Solly, pages 8, 15, 25, 30, 37, 43, 53, 62,
63, 71, 72, 93

Kathy Wilburn, pages 9–14, 22–24, 38–42, 54–55

Eloise Wilken, pages 56–61, 73–92

Cover by David Wenzel

Acknowledgments

*"The Christmas Sleigh Ride" from BACK TO SCHOOL WITH BETSY by Carolyn Haywood,
copyright 1943 by Harcourt Brace Jovanovich, Inc.; renewed 1971 by Carolyn Haywood.
Reprinted by permission of the publisher. "Legends of Christmas" reprinted by permission from
CHRISTMAS PLAYS AND PROGRAMS by Aileen Fisher.
Copyright © 1960, 1970 by Aileen Fisher. Publishers: Plays, Inc., Boston, MA.*

Contents

A Catch by the Hearth

Sing we all merrily
    Christmas is here,
The day we love best
    Of days in the year.

Bring forth the holly,
    The box, and the bay,
Deck out our cottage
    For glad Christmas Day.

Sing we all merrily
    Draw round the fire,
Sister and brother,
    Grandson and sire.

Christmas Eve for Judy and Jerry

It was the day before Christmas. Judy and Jerry were going to town to do their Christmas shopping.

"I wish it could have been any other day," Daddy said as they started. "You know what the city will be like today."

Mother nodded and turned their collars up against the cold and snow. "Yes, I know," she said.

But Judy and Jerry did not know. And they wondered how it would be.

They found out soon enough. The city was bursting with bustle and noise. There were the groaning of buses, and the honking of cabs, and the *chuff-chuff* of snow plows gulping up the snow. And there were people, people everywhere.

All the taxis and buses and trucks honked and hustled. And the people were in such a hurry that they kept bumping into each other and brushing each other's hats with their parcels.

"Oh, my!" said Judy, watching from the car window. "I don't know if I want to shop in the city after all."

"It's not so bad," laughed Daddy as he swung the car into a parking lot. "Just keep close to me, and we'll be all right."

So Judy and Jerry really stuck tight, until a very large man with a great stack of bundles higher than his head came straight toward them like a great big truck.

Judy and Jerry just had to step aside. And when they got past the great big man, Daddy was nowhere to be seen.

They looked all around as hard as they could. There were ladies in green coats with red packages, and ladies in red coats with big brown bundles. There were men in gray coats with their collars pulled over their ears. But no Daddy.

Judy felt a funny lump rising in her throat. "Mommy will never let us come to the city again if we lose Daddy," she said, and her voice sounded choky and strange.

But Jerry had spotted a familiar figure, a white-bearded fellow in a bright red suit. "There!" he cried. "There's one of Santa's helpers. He will help us."

And pulling Judy along by one hand, he pushed his way through the hustling crowd.

"Can you help us find our daddy?" he politely asked.

Santa's helper looked down in surprise. "Lost your daddy, have you?" he asked. "Well, now, that is too bad. I'll certainly do what I can to help. Would that be your daddy coming now?"

And sure enough, there came Daddy, pushing through the crowd straight toward Judy's red tassel cap. "Thank you, Santa," said Daddy when he had the children safely by the hands again.

And away they went into a huge and bright warm store. There was music playing somewhere that they could not see, and there were *so* many presents piled on every side that they felt quite out of breath. But they managed to remember what they had come to buy, and they bought every single thing—a red apron for Mother, a blue scarf for Grandma, a pipe for Daddy (while he turned his back), and secret presents for each other.

With the shopping all finished, they walked along the busy street and looked in the bright windows. Now they didn't mind being jostled and pushed, as long as they were with Daddy.

"How about food?" said Daddy.

And suddenly they knew they were hungry, really starved. So Daddy found a place to eat that was just like a circus tent. And a real clown came to talk to them, too.

"Well, we'd better be off for home," said Daddy when lunch was over. So back they went to the car. And away they rode through the snowy dusk toward home.

When they stopped at the corner Christmas-tree stand to pick up the tree, they knew they were close to home. They waved at some friends who were coasting on the long School Hill.

And then there it was, their very own house, with the candle wreath in the window and Mother at the door. And my, they were glad to be back!

Mother soon had supper on the table, with cocoa steaming hot.

"And how was the day in the city?" she asked.

"Oh, wonderful!" cried both Judy and Jerry. "We ate in a circus tent, and talked to a clown, and we lost Daddy for a little while till Santa's helper found him again, and…" Their words tumbled over each other.

"Well," said Daddy, pushing back his chair, "I have to set the tree up for Santa Claus to trim."

"Oh, we'll help, we'll help," Judy and Jerry cried. But their yawns grew wider, and their eyes began to close.

And Mother said, "Tomorrow is another day."

"Tomorrow's Christmas!" said the children. But as they climbed into bed, after stockings had been tacked up and one sleepy carol sung, they both said together, "But how could Christmas be *better* than our Christmas Eve?"

Christmas in the Country

By Barbara Collyer and John R. Foley

Betty and Bob were going to the country to spend Christmas with Grandmother and Grandfather.

They rode through the snowy countryside. And when they arrived at the station, there was Grandfather, waiting to greet them with a great big sleigh!

There were hugs and kisses all around, and then they all piled into the sleigh. The sleigh bells went *tinkle-tinkle*, the horses went *snort-snort*, and off they rode down the snowy village streets.

Soon they were all greeting Grandmother at the door of the cozy farmhouse. "My, how you've grown!" she said. "Come along now, and get washed up."

"I have some important business with Bob over at the edge of the pasture," Grandfather said.

"What is it? May I come, too?" Betty asked.

"It's a secret," Grandfather said very mysteriously.

"Never you mind, child," Grandmother said. "You come along to the kitchen. I have a secret for you, too."

Chop! Chop! Chop! went the secret in the pasture.

Stitch! Stitch! Stitch! went the secret in the kitchen.

"My secret is round and red, and there's a lot of it," Betty said at the dinner table.

"Mine is big and pointy and smells good," Bob said.

Bob's surprise was standing in a corner of the parlor. It was big and pointy and smelled very good.

It was the Christmas tree!

What a wonderful busy time there was then, with the lights to put on, and the boxes of colored balls, and angels and stars!

And Betty hung her cranberry chain on the tree all by herself!

Then the family gathered around the old piano to sing carols.

But it had been a long, busy day, and Betty's eyes began to close. And before the last notes of "Silent Night" were sung, she was fast asleep in Grandmother's rocker!

So Grandfather carried Betty up to bed. And Grandmother took Bob by the hand.

13

"Grandmother," Bob asked as she tucked him in, "is everybody in the world getting ready for Christmas the way we are?"

"Everybody," Grandmother assured him. "Why I daresay over in the barn at this very moment even the animals are getting ready.

"Perhaps they're having a tree of their own, and of course the hen would be making corn garlands for it, just as Betty made her cranberry chain.

"And the pigs, well, they'd surely be seeing to the goodies for the next day's feast...if they didn't eat them all up themselves first.

"And the cows might be wrapping up presents. My, how handy their horns would be!

"The little lambs, of course, would give the wool for Christmas stockings. Perhaps they'd even learn to knit themselves, since Christmas is a magic time when anything can happen.

"Even the littlest animals do their bit to help, until at last it's time to go to sleep.

"And now it is time for this little one to go to sleep, too. For remember, everywhere—on Christmas Eve—to all good children Santa Claus comes!"

14

The First Nowell

The_ first_ Now - ell the_ an - gel did say Was to
cer - tain poor shep-herds in fields as they lay; In_ fields_ where
they lay_ keep-ing their sheep, On a cold win-ter's night_ that
was_ so deep. Now - ell,_ Now - ell, Now - ell, Nowell._ Born is the King_ of Is - ra - el.

The Peterkins' Christmas Tree

from *The Peterkin Papers*

By Lucretia P. Hale

Early in the autumn the Peterkins began to prepare for their Christmas tree. Everything was done in great privacy as it was to be a surprise to the neighbors, as well as to the rest of the family. Mr. Peterkin had been up to Mr. Bromwick's woodlot, and with his consent, selected the tree. Agamemnon went to look at it occasionally after dark, and Solomon John made frequent visits to it mornings, just after sunrise. Mr. Peterkin drove Elizabeth Eliza and her mother that way, and pointed furtively to it with his whip; but none of them ever spoke of it aloud to each other. It was suspected that the little boys had been to see it Wednesday and Saturday afternoons. But they came home with their pockets full of chestnuts, and said nothing about it.

At length Mr. Peterkin had it cut down and brought secretly into the Larkins' barn. A week or two before Christmas a measurement was made of it with Elizabeth Eliza's yard-measure. To Mr. Peterkin's great dismay it was discovered that it was too high to stand in the back parlor.

This fact was brought out at a secret council of Mr. and Mrs. Peterkin, Elizabeth Eliza, and Agamemnon.

Agamemnon suggested that it might be set up slanting, but Mrs. Peterkin was very sure it would make her dizzy, and the candles would drip.

But a brilliant idea came to Mr. Peterkin. He proposed that the ceiling of the parlor should be raised to make room for the top of the tree.

Elizabeth Eliza thought the space would need to be quite large. It must not be like a small box, or you could not see the tree.

"Yes," said Mr. Peterkin, "I should have the ceiling lifted all across the room; the effect would be finer."

Elizabeth Eliza objected to having the whole ceiling raised, because her room was over the back parlor, and she would have no floor while the alteration was going on, which would be very awkward. Besides, her room was not very high now, and, if the floor were raised, perhaps she could not walk in it upright.

Mr. Peterkin explained that he didn't propose altering the whole ceiling, but to lift up a ridge across the room at the back part where the tree was to stand. This would make a hump, to be sure, in Elizabeth Eliza's room.

Elizabeth Eliza said she would not mind that. It would be like the cuddy thing that comes up on the deck of a ship, that you sit against, only here you would not have the seasickness.

Mrs. Peterkin thought it would come in the worn place of the carpet, and might be a convenience in making the carpet over.

Agamemnon was afraid there would be trouble in keeping the matter secret, for it would be a long piece of work for a carpenter; but Mr. Peterkin proposed having the carpenter for a day or two, for a number of other jobs.

One of them was to make all the chairs in the house of the same height, for Mrs. Peterkin had nearly broken her spine by sitting down in a chair that she had supposed was her own rocking chair, and it had proved to be two inches lower. The little boys were now large enough to sit in any chair; so a medium was fixed upon, and the chairs were made uniformly of the same height.

On consulting the carpenter, however, he insisted that the tree could be cut off at the lower end to suit the height of the parlor, and demurred at so great a change as altering the ceiling. But Mr. Peterkin had set his mind upon the improvement, and Elizabeth Eliza had cut her carpet in preparation for it.

17

So the folding doors into the back parlor were closed, and for nearly a fortnight before Christmas there was great litter of fallen plastering, and laths, and chips, and shavings; and Elizabeth Eliza's carpet was taken up, and the furniture had to be changed, and one night she had to sleep at the Bromwicks', for there was a long hole in her floor that might be dangerous.

All this delighted the little boys. They could not understand what was going on. Perhaps they suspected a Christmas tree, but they did not know why a Christmas tree should have so many chips, and were still more astonished at the hump that appeared in Elizabeth Eliza's room. It must be a Christmas present, or else the tree in a box.

Some aunts and uncles, too, arrived a day or two before Christmas, with some small cousins. These cousins occupied the attention of the little boys, and there was a great deal of whispering and mystery, behind doors, and under the stairs, and in the corners of the entry.

Solomon John was busy, privately making some candles for the tree. He had been collecting some bayberries, as he understood they made very nice candles, so that it would not be necessary to buy any.

The elders of the family all went into the back parlor together, and all tried not to see what was going on. Mrs. Peterkin would go in with Solomon John, or Mr. Peterkin with Elizabeth Eliza, or Elizabeth Eliza and Agamemnon and Solomon John. The little boys and the small cousins were never allowed even to look inside the room.

stretching up into the space arranged for it. All the chips and shavings were cleared away, and it stood on a neat box.

But what were they to put upon the tree?

Solomon John had brought in his supply of candles; but they proved to be very "stringy" and very few of them. It was strange how many bayberries it took to make a few candles! The little boys had helped him, and he had gathered as much as a bushel of bayberries. He had put them in water, and skimmed off the wax, according to the directions; but there was so little wax!

Solomon John had given the little boys some of the bits sawed off from the legs of the chairs. He had suggested that they should cover them with gilt paper, to answer for gilt apples, without telling them what they were for.

These apples, a little blunt at the end, and the candles, were all they had for the tree!

After all her trips into town Elizabeth Eliza had forgotten to bring anything for it.

"I thought of candies and sugar-plums," she said, "but I concluded if we made caramels ourselves we should not need them. But, then, we have not made caramels. The fact is, that day my head was full of my carpet. I had bumped it pretty badly, too."

Mr. Peterkin wished he had taken, instead of a fir tree, an apple tree he had seen in October, full of red fruit.

"But the leaves would have fallen off by this time," said Elizabeth Eliza.

"And the apples, too," said Solomon John.

Elizabeth Eliza meanwhile went into town a number of times. She wanted to consult Amanda as to how much ice cream they should need, and whether they could make it at home, as they had cream and ice. She was pretty busy in her own room; the furniture had to be changed, and the carpet altered. The "hump" was higher than she expected. There was danger of bumping her own head whenever she crossed it. She had to nail some padding on the ceiling for fear of accidents.

The afternoon before Christmas, Elizabeth Eliza, Solomon John, and their father collected in the back parlor for a council. The carpenters had done their work, and the tree stood at its full height at the back of the room, the top

"It is odd I should have forgotten, that day I went in on purpose to get the things," said Elizabeth Eliza, musingly. "But I went from shop to shop, and didn't know exactly what to get. I saw a great many gilt things for Christmas trees, but I knew the little boys were making the gilt apples; there were plenty of candles in the shops, but I knew Solomon John was making the candles."

Mr. Peterkin thought it was quite natural.

Solomon John wondered if it were too late for them to go into town now.

Elizabeth Eliza could not go in the next morning, for there was to be a grand Christmas dinner, and Mr. Peterkin could not be spared, and Solomon John was sure he and Agamemnon would not know what to buy. Besides, they would want to try the candles tonight.

Mr. Peterkin asked if the presents everybody had been preparing would not answer. But Elizabeth Eliza knew they would be too heavy.

A gloom came over the room. There was only a flickering gleam from one of Solomon John's candles that he had lighted by way of trial.

Solomon John again proposed going into town. He lighted a match to examine the newspaper about the trains. There were plenty of trains coming out at that hour, but none going in except a very late one. That would not leave time to do anything and come back.

"We could go in, Elizabeth Eliza and I," said Solomon John, "but we should not have time to buy anything."

Agamemnon was summoned in. Mrs. Peterkin was entertaining the uncles and aunts in the front parlor. Agamemnon wished there was time to study up something about electric lights. If they could only have a calcium light! Solomon John's candle sputtered and went out.

At this moment there was a loud knocking at the front door. The little boys, and the small cousins, and the uncles and aunts, and Mrs. Peterkin hastened to see what was the matter.

The uncles and aunts thought somebody's house must be on fire. The door was opened, and there was a man, white with flakes, for it was beginning to snow, and he was pulling in a large box.

Mrs. Peterkin supposed it contained some of Elizabeth Eliza's purchases, so she ordered it to be pushed into the back parlor, and hastily called back her guests and the little boys into the other room. The little boys and the small cousins were sure they had seen Santa Claus himself.

Mr. Peterkin lighted the gas. The box was addressed to Elizabeth Eliza. It was from her friend from Philadelphia! She had gathered a hint from Elizabeth Eliza's letters that there was to be a Christmas tree, and had filled this box with all that would be needed.

It was opened directly. There was every kind of gilt hanging thing, from gilt peapods to butterflies on springs. There were shining flags and lanterns, and bird cages, and nests with birds sitting on them, baskets of fruit, gilt apples, and bunches of grapes, and, at the bottom of the whole, a large box of candles and a box of Philadelphia bonbons!

Elizabeth Eliza and Solomon John could scarcely keep from screaming. The little boys and the small cousins knocked on the folding doors to ask what was the matter.

Hastily Mr. Peterkin and the rest took out the things and hung them on the tree, and put on the candles.

When all was done, it looked so well that Mr. Peterkin exclaimed: "Let us light the candles now, and send to invite all the neighbors tonight, and have the tree on Christmas Eve!"

And so it was that the Peterkins had their Christmas tree the day before, and on Christmas night could go and visit their neighbors.

21

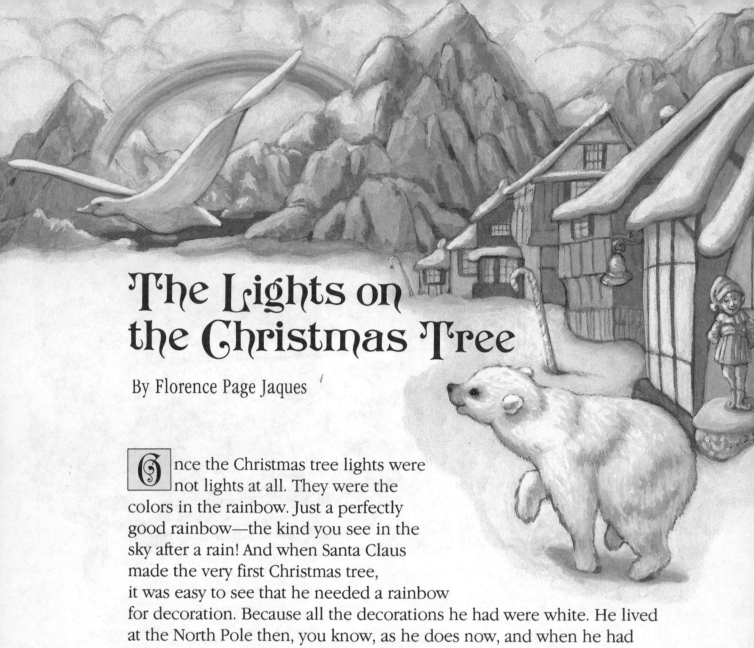

The Lights on the Christmas Tree

By Florence Page Jaques

Once the Christmas tree lights were not lights at all. They were the colors in the rainbow. Just a perfectly good rainbow—the kind you see in the sky after a rain! And when Santa Claus made the very first Christmas tree, it was easy to see that he needed a rainbow for decoration. Because all the decorations he had were white. He lived at the North Pole then, you know, as he does now, and when he had powdered the tree with snow and hung icicles all over it and tied snowballs on the ends of the branches, he looked at it and said:

"No—it's pretty, but it ought to have some color on it. It needs red and green and blue and gold—"

"Oh, Santa Claus," said the Littlest White Bear. "Let's put a rainbow on it!"

"That's just what it needs," Santa Claus agreed. "I'll send the Biggest White Bear to get one."

"Oh!" said the Littlest White Bear. He was so disappointed that the tears came to his eyes. "I was the one who thought of the rainbow. I think you might let me find it!"

"All right then," Santa Claus said kindly. "But you must be *very* careful. Rainbows are easy to break, you know, and really you are the clumsiest, funny little bear."

22

"Oh, I will be careful," promised the Littlest Bear, and he ran and ran on his fat little legs till he found the most beautiful rainbow. Then he picked it and hung it over his back and went home to Santa Claus, walking very carefully. He walked safely past the snow fields and safely past icebergs and safely past the slippery slides, and at last he came to Santa Claus's steps, and saw Santa Claus in the doorway, waiting for him.

"Hurrah!" he laughed, waving his little front paws in triumph. "Here it is!"

And just then both his back feet slipped and—*boom*! He fell on his back, and the rainbow was broken into a thousand pieces.

"Don't cry, don't cry," said Santa Claus, hurrying down the steps. "You aren't hurt!"

"No, but the rainbow is," sobbed the Littlest White Bear, "and I tried so hard to be careful."

"Never you mind." Santa Claus patted him gently. "We'll put the pieces of the rainbow on the tree."

So they picked up a blue piece and put it here, and they picked up a red piece and put it there, and the Christmas tree was prettier than if the rainbow had been all together.

"Oh," said the Littlest White Bear, "I'm glad I fell down!"

And ever since then we have had beautiful rainbow-colored lights on the Christmas tree.

Deck the Halls

Deck the halls with boughs of hol-ly, Fa, la, la, la, la, la, la, la, la. 'Tis the sea-son to be jol-ly, Fa, la, la, la, la, la, la, la, la. Don we now our gay ap-par-el, Fa, la, la, la, la, la, la, la, la. Troll the an-cient yule-tide car-ol, Fa, la, la, la, la, la, la, la, la.

A Visit from Saint Nicholas

By Clement C. Moore

'Twas the night before Christmas, and all through the house
Not a creature was stirring, not even a mouse,
The stockings were hung by the chimney with care,
In hopes that Saint Nicholas soon would be there.
The children were nestled all snug in their beds,
While visions of sugarplums danced in their heads;
And mamma in her kerchief, and I in my cap,
Had just settled down for a long winter's nap,
When out on the lawn there arose such a clatter,
I sprang from the bed to see what was the matter.
Away to the window I flew like a flash,
Tore open the shutters and threw up the sash.
The moon on the breast of the new-fallen snow
Gave the lustre of midday to objects below,
When, what to my wondering eyes should appear,
But a miniature sleigh and eight tiny reindeer,
With a little old driver, so lively and quick
I knew in a moment it must be Saint Nick.

26

More rapid than eagles his coursers they came,
And he whistled and shouted and called them by name.
"Now, Dasher! now, Dancer! now, Prancer! now, Vixen!
On Comet! on Cupid! on Donder and Blitzen!
To the top of the porch, to the top of the wall,
Now dash away, dash away, dash away all!"
As dry leaves that before the wild hurricane fly,
When they meet with an obstacle, mount to the sky,
So up to the housetop the coursers they flew,
With the sleigh full of toys and Saint Nicholas, too;
And then, in a twinkling, I heard on the roof
The prancing and pawing of each tiny hoof.
As I drew in my head and was turning around,
Down the chimney Saint Nicholas came with a bound.

He was dressed all in fur from his head to his foot,
And his clothes were all tarnished with ashes and soot;
A bundle of toys he had flung on his back,
And he looked like a peddler just opening his pack.
His eyes, how they twinkled! his dimples, how merry!
His cheeks were like roses, his nose like a cherry,
His droll little mouth was drawn up like a bow,
And the beard on his chin was as white as the snow;
The stump of a pipe he held tight in his teeth,
And the smoke, it encircled his head like a wreath.
He had a broad face and a round little belly
That shook, when he laughed, like a bowl full of jelly.

He was chubby and plump, a right jolly old elf.
And I laughed when I saw him, in spite of myself.
A wink of his eye and a twist of his head
Soon gave me to know I had nothing to dread.
He spoke not a word, but went straight to his work,
And filled all the stockings—then turned with a jerk,
And laying a finger aside of his nose,
And giving a nod, up the chimney he rose.
He sprang to his sleigh, to his team gave a whistle,
And away they all flew like the down of a thistle;
But I heard him exclaim, ere he drove out of sight,
"Happy Christmas to all and to all a good night."

Visit

By Kathryn Jackson

Ride up in the elevator—
What floor?
Toys!

Line up in the eager throng of
Girls and
Boys—

Move up close and closer, past the
Christmas
Tree—

Your turn! It's your turn to sit on
Santa's
Knee!

A Kidnapped Santa Claus

From the story by L. Frank Baum

Santa Claus lives in the Laughing Valley, where stands the big rambling castle in which his toys are manufactured. His workmen, selected from the ryls, knooks, pixies, and fairies, live with him, and every one is as busy as can be from one year's end to another.

On one side of the Valley is the mighty Forest of Burzee. At the other side stands the huge mountain that contains the Caves of the Daemons.

One would think that our good old Santa Claus, who devotes his days to making children happy, would have no enemies on all the earth. But the Daemons who live in the mountain caves grew to hate Santa Claus very much, and all for the simple reason that he made children happy.

Well, these Daemons, thinking they had cause to dislike Santa Claus, held a meeting to discuss the matter. They knew that Santa Claus worked all through the year at his castle in the Laughing Valley, preparing the gifts he was to distribute on Christmas Eve.

And it is well known that no harm can come to Santa Claus while he is in the Laughing Valley, for the fairies, and ryls, and knooks all protect him. But on Christmas Eve he drives his reindeer out into the big world, carrying a sleigh-load of toys and pretty gifts to the children; and this was the time and the occasion when his enemies had the best chance to injure him. So the Daemons laid their plans and awaited the arrival of Christmas Eve.

The moon shone big and white in the sky, and the snow lay crisp and sparkling on the ground as Santa Claus cracked his whip and sped away out of the Valley into the great world beyond. The roomy sleigh was packed full with huge sacks of toys, and as the reindeer dashed onward our jolly old Santa laughed and whistled and sang for very joy. For in all his merry life this was the one day in the year when he was happiest—the day he lovingly bestowed the treasures of his workshop upon the little children.

Suddenly a strange thing happened: A rope shot through the moonlight and a big noose that was in the end of it settled over the arms and body of Santa Claus and drew tight. Before he could resist or even cry out he was jerked from the seat of the sleigh and tumbled head foremost into a snowbank, while the reindeer rushed onward with the load of toys and carried it quickly out of sight and sound.

Such a surprising experience con-fused old Santa for a moment, and when he had collected his senses he found that the wicked Daemons had pulled him from the snowdrift and bound him tightly with many coils of the stout rope. And then they carried the kidnapped Santa Claus away to their mountain, where they thrust the prisoner into a secret cave and chained him to the rocky wall so that he could not escape.

"Ha, ha!" laughed the Daemons, rubbing their hands together with cruel glee. "What will the children do now?"

Now it so chanced that on this Christmas Eve the good Santa Claus had taken with him in his sleigh Nuter the Ryl, Peter the Knook, Kilter the Pixie, and a small fairy named Wisk—his four favorite assistants. These little people he had often found very useful in helping him to distribute his gifts to the children, and when their master was so suddenly dragged from the sleigh they were all snugly tucked underneath the seat, where the sharp wind could not reach them.

Little Wisk stuck out his head from underneath the seat and found Santa Claus gone and no one to direct the flight of the reindeer.

"Whoa!" he called out, and the deer obediently came to a halt.

Peter and Nuter and Kilter all jumped upon the seat and looked back over the track made by the sleigh. But Santa Claus had been left miles and miles behind.

"What shall we do?" asked Wisk, anxiously, all the mirth and mischief banished from his wee face by this great calamity.

"We must go back at once and find our master," said Nuter the Ryl, who thought and spoke with much deliberation.

"No, no!" exclaimed Peter the Knook, who, cross and crabbed though he was, might always be depended upon in an emergency. "If we delay, or go back, there will not be time to get the toys to the children before morning; and that would grieve Santa Claus more than anything else."

"It is certain that some wicked creatures have captured him," added Kilter, thoughtfully, "and their object must be to make the children unhappy. So our first duty is to get the toys distributed as carefully as if Santa Claus were himself present. Afterward we can search for our master and easily secure his freedom."

This seemed such good and sensible advice that the others at once resolved to adopt it. So Peter the Knook called to the reindeer, and the faithful animals again sprang forward and dashed over hill and valley, through forest and plain, until they came to the houses wherein children lay sleeping and dreaming of the pretty gifts they would find on Christmas morning.

The little immortals had set themselves a difficult task; for although they had assisted Santa Claus on many of his journeys, their master had always directed and guided them and told them exactly what he wished them to do. But now they had to distribute the toys according to their own judgment, and they did not understand children as well as did old Santa. So it is no wonder they made some laughable errors.

Mamie Brown, who wanted a doll, got a drum instead; and a drum is of no use to a girl who loves dolls. And Charlie Smith, who delights to romp and play out of doors, and who wanted some new rubber boots to keep his feet dry, received a sewing-box filled with colored worsteds and threads and needles, which made him so provoked that he thoughtlessly called our dear Santa Claus a fraud.

Had there been many such mistakes the Daemons would have accomplished their evil purpose and made the children unhappy. But the little friends of the absent Santa Claus labored faithfully and intelligently to carry out their master's ideas, and they made fewer errors than might be expected under such unusual circumstances.

And, although they worked as swiftly as possible, day had begun to break before the toys and other presents were all distributed; so for the first time in many years the reindeer trotted into the Laughing Valley, on their return, in broad daylight, with the brilliant sun peeping over the edge of the forest to prove they were far behind their accustomed hour.

Having put the deer in the stable, the little folk began to wonder how they might rescue their master; and they realized they must discover, first of all, what had happened to him and where he was.

When Christmas Day dawned the Daemon of Malice was guarding Santa Claus, and his tongue was sharp. "The children are waking up, Santa!" he cried. "They are waking up to find their stockings empty! Ho, ho! How they will quarrel, and wail, and stamp their feet in anger!"

But to this, as to other like taunts, Santa Claus answered nothing. He was much grieved by his capture, it is true; but his courage did not forsake him. And, finding that the prisoner would not reply to his jeers, the Daemon of Malice presently went away, and sent the Daemon of Repentance to take his place.

"It is morning now," said he, as he entered the cavern, "and the mischief is done. You cannot visit the children again for another year."

34

"That is true," answered Santa Claus, almost cheerfully. "Christmas Eve is past, and for the first time in centuries I have not visited my children."

"The little ones will be greatly disappointed," murmured the Daemon of Repentance, almost regretfully, "but that cannot be helped now. I am even now repenting that I assisted in your capture. And to prove that I sincerely regret my share in your capture I am going to permit you to escape."

The fellow at once busied himself untying the knots that bound Santa Claus. Then he led the way through a long tunnel.

"I hope you will forgive me," said the Daemon, pleadingly. "I am not really a bad person, you know."

With this he opened a back door that let in a flood of sunshine, and Santa Claus sniffed the fresh air gratefully.

"I bear no malice," said he to the Daemon, in a gentle voice. "So good morning, and a Merry Christmas to you!"

With these words he stepped out to greet the bright morning, and a moment later he was trudging along, whistling softly to himself, on his way to his home in the Laughing Valley.

Marching over the snow toward the mountain was a vast army, made up of the most curious creatures imaginable. There were numberless knooks from the forest, as rough and crooked in appearance as the gnarled branches of the trees they ministered to. And there were dainty ryls from the fields, each one bearing the emblem of the flower or plant it guarded. Behind these were many ranks of pixies, gnomes, and nymphs, and in the rear a thousand beautiful fairies floating along in gorgeous array.

This wonderful army was led by Wisk, Peter, Nuter, and Kilter, who had assembled it to rescue Santa Claus from captivity and to punish those who had dared to take him away.

But lo! coming to meet his loyal friends appeared the imposing form of Santa Claus, his white beard floating in the breeze and his bright eyes sparkling at this proof of the love and veneration he had inspired in the hearts of the most powerful creatures in existence.

And while they clustered around him and danced with glee at his safe return, he gave them earnest thanks for their support. But Wisk, and Nuter, and Peter, and Kilter he embraced affectionately.

So the fairies, and knooks, and pixies, and ryls all escorted the good man to his castle, and there left him to talk over the events of the night with his little assistants.

Wisk had already rendered himself invisible and flown through the big world to see how the children were getting along on this bright Christmas morning; and by the time he returned, Peter had finished telling Santa Claus of how they had distributed the toys.

"We really did very well," cried the Fairy, in a pleased voice, "for I found little unhappiness among the children this morning. Still, you must not get captured again, my dear master, for we might not be so fortunate another time in carrying out your ideas."

He then related the mistakes that had been made, and which he had not discovered until his tour of inspection. And Santa Claus at once sent him with rubber boots for Charlie Smith, and a doll for Mamie Brown; so that even those two disappointed ones became happy.

Jingle Bells

Music by James Pierpont

Jin - gle bells, Jin - gle bells, Jin - gle all the way!

Oh, what fun it is to ride in a one-horse o - pen sleigh!__

Jin - gle bells, Jin - gle bells, Jin - gle all the way!

Oh, what fun it is to ride in a one-horse o - pen sleigh!

The Christmas Sleigh Ride
from *Back to School with Betsy*
By Carolyn Haywood

A few days before Christmas Father said that he had a surprise.

Betsy shouted, "I bet I know! It's a sleigh ride!"

"Yes," said Father. "If the snow lasts, I have arranged for a sleighing party. It will be on Christmas Eve. You can invite five of the children from school."

"Oh, Father!" cried Betsy. "It's wonderful! Will we go sleighing in the park?"

"Yes," said Father, "in the park."

Betsy invited Billy and Ellen and Christopher, Mary Lou and Peter.

Betsy told the children about Father's dream when he was a little boy.

"Oh, boy!" said Billy. "I wish I could go sleigh riding with Santa Claus, the way your father did."

When Christmas Eve arrived, the snow was packed hard on the roads. It was so hard and frozen that it was shiny and made a squeaky noise. The night was clear and the stars seemed brighter than ever to Betsy.

By seven o'clock the children were all at Betsy's house. Father put them into the car and drove them to a livery stable near the park. In front of the stable there was a big sleigh with two horses. The sleigh had a high seat for the driver and two wide seats behind that faced each other.

"Now, Billy and Ellen can ride with the driver first," said Father. "Then Christopher and Mary Lou can have a turn, and on the way back Peter and Betsy can ride up front."

This satisfied the children and they scrambled into the sleigh. Father tucked the rugs around them. The horses stamped their feet and shook their heads. The sleigh bells jingled.

"Are you going to drive the sleigh, Father?" asked Betsy.

"Oh, my, no!" said Father, as he climbed into the back seat beside Betsy. "The driver will be here in a moment."

"I wish we were going for a sleigh ride with Santa Claus, the way you did in your dream," said Billy.

No sooner had Billy said this than the door of the stable opened. Who should walk out but Santa Claus! He was wearing a bright red suit and cap trimmed with fur and he had on high black boots. The sleigh bells around his waist jingled as he walked.

"Hello, boys and girls!" he shouted.

"So you're going for a ride with me tonight!"

The children could hardly believe their eyes. They were speechless as Santa Claus climbed up into the driver's seat and took the reins in his hands.

"Gee up!" said Santa Claus to the horses.

The sleigh started with a lurch. They were off!

Billy was the first to find his tongue. He said, "Are you really Santa Claus?"

"Sure, me boy, I'm his twin brother," replied Santa Claus, "and just as good. He'd 'a' come himself but he's having a big night tonight getting up and down chimneys."

"Do you live at the North Pole?" asked Mary Lou.

"Not me!" said Santa Claus. "It's too cold. My whiskers freeze."

"Don't you have to help your brother on Christmas Eve?" asked Christopher.

"No," replied Santa Claus, "I never was any good getting up and down chimneys. Always seemed sort of round-about to me, but me brother's all for it. Did it even as a little fellow. Never would come in through the door like other folks."

The children laughed very hard and asked a great many questions. They were driving through the park now. It was very quiet. There was no sound but the sound of the sleigh bells. Betsy looked up at the tall trees. The stars peeped between the branches and winked at her. In the distance she could hear other sleigh bells. She burrowed down into the warm rugs and held Father's hand. She felt all happy inside. Betsy hadn't known that a sleigh ride could be so wonderful.

"Let's sing 'Jingle Bells,'" shouted Billy.

They all sang.

"'Jingle bells, jingle bells,
  Jingle all the way.
  Oh, what fun it is to ride
  In a one-horse open sleigh.'"

"Let's sing 'two-horse open sleigh,'" said Christopher. "'Cause that is what this sleigh is."

So then they all sang, "'Oh, what fun it is to ride in a two-horse open sleigh.'"

All of a sudden the horses changed their gait. The sleigh jolted and Billy toppled right off the front seat. He went head first into a big snowdrift.

"Whoa!" cried Santa Claus, as he pulled up the horses.

The sleigh stopped and Betsy's father jumped down. He ran back to Billy. The children turned around to see where Billy was. All that they could see were two legs covered with dark green snowpants sticking out of the snowdrift. The legs were kicking furiously.

In a moment Father had pulled Billy out. He looked very much like the snowman in Betsy's garden.

Father brushed him off and they ran back to the sleigh.

"I fell out," said Billy, when he reached the sleigh.

"You don't mean to tell me!" said Santa Claus. "Sure, and I thought you were practicing diving."

The children changed places in the sleigh. Christopher and Mary Lou sat up with Santa Claus while Billy and Ellen took seats in the back of the sleigh.

"It's funny," said Christopher to Santa Claus, "but you talk just like Mr. Kilpatrick."

"Yes, you do," cried the rest of the children, "just exactly like Mr. Kilpatrick."

"And who may Mr. Kilpatrick be?" asked Santa.

"Mr. Kilpatrick is the policeman who takes us across the street," said Betsy.

"Oh, that fellow!" shouted Santa Claus. "Sure, I've seen him often. He's got a face like a dish of turnips and hair the color of carrots."

The children laughed. "I don't think it's nice of you to talk about Mr. Kilpatrick that way," said Ellen.

"Sure, there's nobody with a better right," said Santa Claus.

"I think you *are* Mr. Kilpatrick," said Mary Lou.

"'Kilpatrick!' What a name!" said Santa Claus. "Upon my word, I've killed flies and I've killed mosquitoes, but never have I killed any Patrick."

The children shouted with laughter.

By this time the sleigh had reached a house. It stood by the road under tall trees. Lights shone from the windows. It was an old inn.

Santa Claus stopped the sleigh and everyone climbed down. A boy in the yard led the horses to a shed nearby.

Santa Claus led the way into the inn. There was a fire roaring in the fireplace.

Betsy's eyes were as big as saucers. "Why, Father, it's just like your dream when you were a little boy," she said.

In front of the fireplace there was a table. They all sat down at the table. Santa Claus sat at the head of the table.

"Are we going to have something to eat?" asked Billy.

"We certainly are," said Santa Claus. "What do you want to eat, Billy?"

"Hot dogs," shouted Billy at the top of his voice.

"Yes, hot dogs!" shouted all of the children except Betsy. She was laughing so hard she couldn't say anything. At last she said, "Oh, Father!" and she began laughing again. "Do you remember the hot dogs in your dream?"

Father laughed, too. "Yes," he said, "I remember."

After the children had eaten their hot dogs and drunk big cups of cocoa, they went out to the sleigh. They felt all warmed up.

When they were settled, with Betsy and Peter on the front seat with Santa Claus, they started for home.

Jingle, jingle, jingle, went the sleigh bells. *Trot, trot, trot,* went the horses' feet.

Santa Claus joked with the children all the way back to the stable. There the children climbed out. They all shook hands with Santa Claus and thanked him for the lovely sleigh ride.

As they got into Father's car, they cried, "Good night, Santa Claus! Good night and Merry Christmas!"

"Merry Christmas!" shouted Santa Claus. "Remember me to Mr. Kilpatrick!"

"Sure!" shouted Billy. "Remember me to your twin brother."

Father dropped the children off, one by one, at their homes.

"Good night!" they each called. "Thank you and a Merry Christmas!"

When Betsy kissed Father good night, she said, "Father, was Santa Claus Mr. Kilpatrick?"

Father laughed. "Well, what do you think?" he said.

Carol

from *The Wind in the Willows*
By Kenneth Grahame

Villagers all, this frosty tide,
Let your doors swing open wide,
Though wind may follow, and snow beside,
Yet draw us in by your fire to bide;
    Joy shall be yours in the morning!

Here we stand in the cold and the sleet,
Blowing fingers and stamping feet,
Come from far away you to greet—
You by the fire and we in the street—
    Bidding you joy in the morning!

For ere one half of the night was gone,
Sudden a star has led us on,
Raining bliss and benison—
Bliss tomorrow and more anon,
    Joy for every morning!

Goodman Joseph toiled through the snow—
Saw the star o'er a stable low;
Mary she might not further go—
Welcome thatch, and litter below!
    Joy was hers in the morning!

And then they heard the angels tell
"Who were the first to cry Nowell?
Animals all, as it befell,
In the stable where they did dwell!
    Joy shall be theirs in the morning!"

The Twelve Days of Christmas

An Old English Carol

The first day of Christmas,
My true love sent to me
A partridge in a pear tree.

The second day of Christmas,
My true love sent to me
Two turtledoves, and
A partridge in a pear tree.

The third day of Christmas,
My true love sent to me
Three French hens,
Two turtledoves, and
A partridge in a pear tree.

The fourth day of Christmas,
My true love sent to me
Four calling birds,
Three French hens,
Two turtledoves, and
A partridge in a pear tree.

The fifth day of Christmas,
My true love sent to me
Five gold rings,
Four calling birds,
Three French hens,
Two turtledoves, and
A partridge in a pear tree.

The sixth day of Christmas,
My true love sent to me
Six geese a-laying,
Five gold rings,
Four calling birds,
Three French hens,
Two turtledoves, and
A partridge in a pear tree.

The seventh day of Christmas,
My true love sent to me
Seven swans a-swimming,
Six geese a-laying,
Five gold rings,
Four calling birds,
Three French hens,
Two turtledoves, and
A partridge in a pear tree.

The eighth day of Christmas,
My true love sent to me
Eight maids a-milking,
Seven swans a-swimming,
Six geese a-laying,
Five gold rings,
Four calling birds,
Three French hens,
Two turtledoves, and
A partridge in a pear tree.

The ninth day of Christmas,
My true love sent to me
Nine drummers drumming,
Eight maids a-milking,
Seven swans a-swimming,
Six geese a-laying,
Five gold rings,
Four calling birds,
Three French hens,
Two turtledoves, and
A partridge in a pear tree.

The tenth day of Christmas,
My true love sent to me
Ten pipers piping,
Nine drummers drumming,
Eight maids a-milking,
Seven swans a-swimming,
Six geese a-laying,
Five gold rings,
Four calling birds,
Three French hens,
Two turtledoves, and
A partridge in a pear tree.

The eleventh day of Christmas,
My true love sent to me
Eleven ladies dancing,
Ten pipers piping,
Nine drummers drumming,
Eight maids a-milking,
Seven swans a-swimming,
Six geese a-laying,

Five gold rings,
Four calling birds,
Three French hens,
Two turtledoves, and
A partridge in a pear tree.

The twelfth day of Christmas,
My true love sent to me
Twelve fiddlers fiddling,
Eleven ladies dancing,
Ten pipers piping,
Nine drummers drumming,
Eight maids a-milking,
Seven swans a-swimming,
Six geese a-laying,
Five gold rings,
Four calling birds,
Three French hens,
Two turtledoves, and
A partridge in a pear tree.

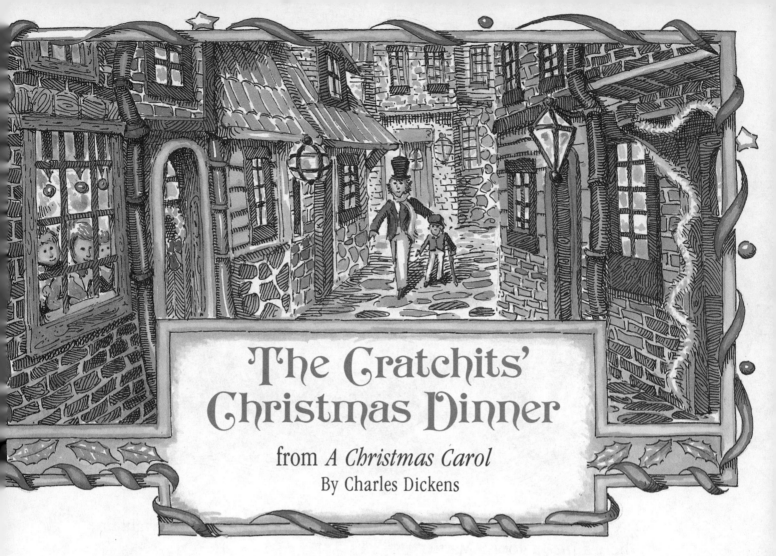

The Cratchits' Christmas Dinner

from *A Christmas Carol*
By Charles Dickens

Then up rose Mrs. Cratchit, Cratchit's wife, dressed out but poorly in a twice-turned gown, but brave in ribbons, which are cheap and make a goodly show for sixpence; and she laid the cloth, assisted by Belinda Cratchit, second of her daughters, also brave in ribbons; while Master Peter Cratchit plunged a fork into the saucepan of potatoes, and getting the corners of his monstrous shirt collar (Bob's private property, conferred upon his son and heir in honor of the day) into his mouth, rejoiced to find himself so gallantly attired, and yearned to show his linen in the fashionable parks. And now two smaller Cratchits, boy and girl, came tearing in, screaming that outside the baker's they had smelled the goose and known it for their own; and basking in luxurious thoughts of sage-and-onion, these young Cratchits danced about the table and exalted Master Peter Cratchit to the skies, while he (not proud, although his collar nearly choked him) blew the fire, until the slow potatoes bubbling up knocked loudly at the saucepan-lid to be let out and peeled.

"What has ever got your precious father then?" said Mrs. Cratchit. "And your brother, Tiny Tim! And Martha wasn't as late last Christmas Day by half-an-hour!"

"Here's Martha, Mother!" cried the two young Cratchits. "Hurrah! There's *such* a goose, Martha!"

"Why, bless your heart alive, my dear, how late you are!" said Mrs. Cratchit, kissing her a dozen times, and taking off her shawl and bonnet for her with officious zeal.

"We'd a deal of work to finish up last night," replied the girl, "and had to clear away this morning, Mother."

"Well! Never mind so long as you are come," said Mrs. Cratchit. "Sit ye down before the fire, my dear, and have a warm, Lord bless ye!"

"No, no! There's Father coming," cried the two young Cratchits, who were everywhere at once. "Hide, Martha, hide!"

So Martha hid herself, and in came little Bob, the father, with at least three feet of comforter exclusive of the fringe, hanging down before him; and his threadbare clothes darned and brushed, to look seasonable; and Tiny Tim upon his shoulder. Alas, for Tiny Tim, he bore a little crutch, and had his limbs supported by an iron frame.

"Why, where's our Martha?" cried Bob Cratchit, looking around.

"Not coming," said Mrs. Cratchit.

"Not coming!" said Bob, with a sudden declension of his high spirits; for he had been Tim's good horse all the way from church, and had come home rampant. "Not coming upon Christmas Day!"

Martha didn't like to see him disappointed, if it were only in joke; so she came out prematurely from behind the closet door, and ran into his arms, while the two young Cratchits hustled Tiny Tim, and bore him off into the wash-house, that he might hear the pudding singing in the copper.

"And how did little Tim behave?" asked Mrs. Cratchit, when she had rallied Bob on his credulity, and Bob had hugged his daughter to his heart's content.

"As good as gold," said Bob, "and better. Somehow he gets thoughtful, sitting by himself so much, and thinks the strangest things you ever heard. He told me, coming home, that he hoped the people saw him in the church because he was a cripple, and it might be pleasant to them to remember upon Christmas Day, who made lame beggars walk and blind men see."

Bob's voice was tremulous when he told them this, and trembled more when he said that Tiny Tim was growing strong and hearty.

His active little crutch was heard upon the floor, and back came Tiny Tim before another word was spoken, escorted by his brother and sister to his stool before the fire; and while Bob, turning up his cuffs— as if, poor fellow, they were capable of being made more shabby— compounded some hot mixture in a jug with gin and lemons, and stirred it round and round and put it on the hob to simmer, Master Peter and the two ubiquitous young Cratchits went to fetch the goose, with which they soon returned in high procession.

Such a bustle ensued that you might have thought a goose the rarest of birds; a feathered phenomenon, to which a black swan was a matter of course—and in truth it was something very like it in that house. Mrs. Cratchit made the gravy (ready beforehand in a little saucepan) hissing hot; Master Peter mashed the potatoes with incredible vigor; Miss Belinda sweetened up the applesauce; Martha dusted the hot plates; Bob took Tiny Tim beside him in a corner at the table; the two young Cratchits set chairs for everyone, not forgetting themselves, and mounting guard upon their posts, crammed spoons into their mouths, lest they should shriek for goose before their turn came to be helped. At last the dishes were set on, and grace was said. It was succeeded by a breathless pause, as Mrs. Cratchit, looking slowly all along the carving-knife, prepared to plunge it in the breast; but when she did, and when the long expected gush of stuffing issued forth, one murmur of delight arose round the boards, and even Tiny Tim, excited by the young Cratchits, beat on the table with the handle of his knife, and feebly cried, "Hurrah!"

There never was such a goose. Bob said he didn't believe there ever was such a goose cooked. Its tenderness and flavor, size and cheapness, were the themes of universal admiration. Eked out by the applesauce and mashed potatoes, it was a sufficient dinner for the whole family; indeed, as Mrs. Cratchit said with great delight (surveying one small atom of bone upon the dish) they hadn't ate it all at last! Yet every one had had enough, and the youngest Cratchits, in particular, were steeped in sage and onions to the eyebrows! But now, the plates being changed by Miss Belinda, Mrs. Cratchit left the room alone—too nervous to bear witnesses—to take the pudding up and bring it in.

Suppose it should not be done enough! Suppose it should break in the turning out! Suppose somebody should have got over the wall of the backyard, and stole it while they were merry with the goose—a supposition at which the two young Cratchits became livid! All sorts of horrors were supposed.

Hallo! A great deal of steam! The pudding was out of the copper. A smell like a washing-day! That was the cloth. A smell like an eating-house and a pastry-cook's next door to each other, with a laundress's next door to that! That was the pudding! In half a minute Mrs. Cratchit entered—flushed, but smiling proudly—with the pudding like a speckled cannonball so hard and firm, blazing in half-a-quartern of ignited brandy, and bedight with Christmas holly stuck into the top.

Oh, a wonderful pudding! Bob Cratchit said, and calmly, too, that he regarded it as the greatest success achieved by Mrs. Cratchit since their marriage. Mrs. Cratchit said that now the weight was off her mind, she would confess she had had her doubts about the quantity of flour. Everybody had something to say about it, but nobody said or thought it was at all a small pudding for a large family. It would have been flat heresy to do so. Any Cratchit would have blushed to hint at such a thing.

At last the dinner was all done, the cloth was cleaned, the hearth swept, and the fire made up. The compound in the jug being tasted, and considered perfect, apples and oranges were put upon the table, and a shovelful of chestnuts on the fire. Then all the Cratchit family drew round the hearth, in what Bob Cratchit called a circle, meaning half a one; and at Bob Cratchit's elbow stood the family display of glass. Two tumblers, and a custard cup without a handle.

These held the hot stuff from the jug, however, as well as golden goblets would have done; and Bob served it out with beaming looks, while the chestnuts on the fire sputtered and cracked noisily. Then Bob proposed:

"A Merry Christmas to us all, my dears. God bless us!"

Which all the family re-echoed.

"God bless us every one!" said Tiny Tim, the last of all.

The Birds' Christmas

"Jay! Jay!" screamed the bluejays. "A fine way to treat us."

"Chick! Chick!" called the black-capped chickadees.

"Tsip! Tsip!" the purple finches cried.

The noisy sparrows made a great racket, too. "Twitter! Twitter!" they scolded. But even their chatter did not bring Jill and Steven to the window with supper for their bird friends. The children were out doing their Christmas shopping.

Soon it grew dark, and it was bedtime for Jill and Steven, and for their bird friends, too.

When the birds woke up the next morning, it was Christmas Day. They flew straight to Jill and Steven's window. The children were there, with a shiny new feeding tray filled with

acorns for the bluejays,

suet for the chickadees,

grain for the purple finches,

and a little bit of everything for the sparrows.

"Merry Christmas, bird friends," Jill and Steven called out. "We didn't forget you! We were shopping for your Christmas present. Do you like it?"

"Jay! Jay!" "Twitter! Twitter!" "Chick! Chick!" "Tsip! Tsip!" the birds sang back happily between nibbles.

And if you understand bird talk, you know that they meant, "Merry Christmas to you. This is the best Christmas present ever!"

Round the Year to Christmas

In the **spring**, Christmas seems a long time away. But the lambs and the sheep are feeding in the pasture so their wool will be long and thick for Christmas socks and mittens.

The apple and plum trees are in blossom for Christmas fruit. And Farmer Brown has planted seeds in the soft brown earth of the garden plot. Christmas is coming—but a long way off.

As spring turns into **summer**, Christmas comes closer. Farmer Brown tends the fruits and the vegetables that Mother will fix for Christmas dinner. Small green apples and plums appear on the trees.

The sheep and the lambs are shorn of their wool, so it can be made into yarn. But the children and cows nap in the warm shade, with scarcely a thought of winter's cold joys. For it is still a long time till Christmas.

Autumn is here. Now the fruits of the summer are gathered in—the squash and potatoes and onions and such. Farmer Brown and his wife harvest golden corn and fat orange pumpkins—some for scary jack-o'-lanterns, some for holiday pumpkin pies. The apples are red now, and the plums deep blue, and all ripe for the pickers.

Down in the woodlot the Christmas tree stands green and full among the fading autumn trees. And in the busy kitchen plum puddings are made, and the rosiest apples set aside for Christmas stocking toes. For Christmas is not such a long time away.

It is **winter** now. Snow is on the ground, and the children are sledding on the garden slopes. Christmas is just one day off.

Inside the farmhouse Mother Brown is baking pies for Christmas dinner. Tomorrow everyone will eat his fill of turkey or of goose. There will be presents to open and friends to see.

And then Christmas will be over—but not for long. For soon spring will be here again, and in the garden and meadows all over the farm a new Christmas will be growing.

Christmas ABC

By Florence Johnson

A is for angels
from Heaven above.

B is for bells,
ringing news
of God's love.

C is for Christmas,
our most joyful day.

D is for Dancer,
who pulls Santa's sleigh.

E is for evergreen,
a fine Christmas tree.

F is for flower,
so pretty to see.

G is for gifts
for our friends
big and tiny.

H is for holly
with leaves
green and shiny.

I is icicles,
agleam in
the sun.

J is for Jesus,
the Holiest One.

K is for kitten,
a warm Christmas ball.

L is for lamp,
a bright welcome
to all.

M is for mailbox
with mail
overflowing.

 is for neighbors,
their cold faces glowing.

is for ornaments,
cheery and gleaming.

 is plum pudding,
delicious and steaming.

is for quilt
for a long
winter's nap.

is for ribbon,
your presents to wrap.

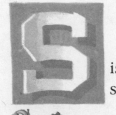 **S** is for Santa Claus,
stockings, and sleigh.

T is for tree,
shining on Christmas Day.

 **U** is for underwear
for when Santa lazes.

V is for voices,
singing carols and praises.

W is for wreath
in front of our house.

X is for kisses
to Santa Claus Mouse.

Y is for Yuletide,
the time of good
cheer.

Z is for *zoom*!
Santa'll be back
next year.

Stocking Song
on Christmas Eve

By Mary Mapes Dodge

Welcome Christmas! heel
  and toe,
Here we wait thee in a row.
Come, good Santa Claus, we beg,
Fill us tightly, foot and leg.

Fill us quickly ere you go,—
Fill us till we overflow,
That's the way! and leave us more
Heaped in piles upon the floor.

Little feet that ran all day
Twitch in dreams of merry play,
Little feet that jumped at will
Lie all pink and white and still.

See us, how we lightly swing,
Hear us, how we try to sing,
Welcome Christmas! heel and toe,
Come and fill us ere you go!

Here we hang till someone nimbly
Jumps with treasures down the chimney.
Bless us! how he'll tickle us!
Funny old Saint Nicholas.

O Christmas Tree

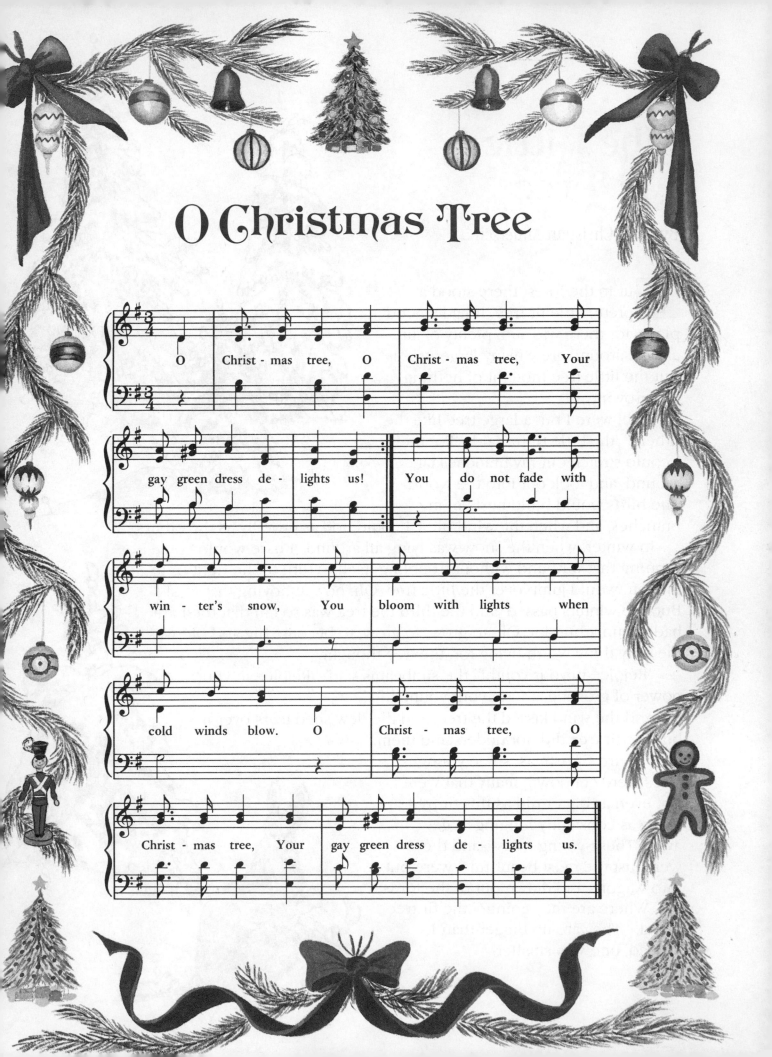

The Little Fir Tree

By Hans Christian Andersen

Out in the forest there stood a pretty little fir tree. It had a good place, for there was sun, plenty of air, and all around grew many larger trees. But the little tree thought of nothing but growing.

"Oh, were I but a large tree like the others!" the little thing said. "For then I could stretch out my branches far around, and look out into the world. The birds would build nests in my branches, and when the wind blew I could nod as proudly as the others."

In winter, when the snow was lying all around, a hare would come running that way, and without troubling itself to turn to the right or to the left, would jump over the little tree. Oh, how annoying that was! But two winters passed, and the third the tree was so tall that the hare had to run around it. Oh, to grow, to grow, to become big and old was the only thing worth living for, the tree thought.

"Rejoice in your youth!" the sunbeams said. "Rejoice in your power of growing, and in your young life."

And the wind kissed the tree, and the dew shed tears over it, but the fir tree did not understand them.

Toward Christmas, some young trees were cut down, many that were not even as big or old as this fir tree that was constantly longing to get away. These young trees—and they were just the most beautiful—were put into wagons and drawn out of the forest.

"Where are they going?" the fir tree asked. "They are no bigger than I. Indeed, one was smaller."

"We know all about that," the sparrows twittered. "Down there in the town we were looking through the windows of the houses, and we know where the young trees are taken. Oh, the greatest splendor awaits them! When we looked through the windows we saw that they were stood up in the middle of the warm room, and adorned with the most beautiful things— gingerbread, gilt apples, playthings of all sorts, and hundreds of wax tapers!"

"And then?" the fir tree asked. "What happens then?"

"We did not see more, but that was very beautiful."

"I wonder whether I shall enjoy all this splendor," the fir tree thought. "Oh, were it but Christmastime! For I am now as tall and stretch out as far as those that were carried away last year. Oh, were I but on the wagon! Were I but in the warm room with all the splendor! And then…yes, then something better and more beautiful must come, or why should they adorn me so? Oh, yes! Something far better must follow. But what?"

"Rejoice in us!" the air and light cried. "Rejoice in your youth, out in the open air!"

But it did not rejoice at all. It just grew and grew. And when Christmas came, it was the very first to be cut down. And as the tree fell, it could not think of any happiness, for it was sad at having to leave the place of its birth, and it was sad that it would never see the other trees again, nor the little bushes, nor the flowers that grew around it, nor even the birds.

The tree did not feel better till it was being unpacked with the others, and it heard a man say, "This is a magnificent one! We shall not want any other."

65

Two servants then came out and carried the fir tree into a large and beautiful room. The tree was put into a large tub filled with sand. Oh, how the tree trembled. What was going to happen now? The servants helped the young ladies to decorate it. They hung little paper baskets upon the branches, and each basket was filled with sweets. Gilt apples and walnuts hung there as if they had grown on the tree, and more than a hundred little red, blue, and white tapers were fixed among the branches. Dolls, exactly like human beings, were swinging through the air, and at the very top of the tree there was a star of gold tinsel. It was truly beautiful!

"Oh, were it but night," the tree thought, "and the tapers lit! And what will happen then, I wonder? Will the other trees come from the forest to see me, and the sparrows fly against the panes of glass? I should like to know whether I shall grow here and remain decorated like this summer and winter."

It thought and thought till its bark ached, and that is the same for a tree as a headache for us.

The tapers were now lit. What splendor! The branches of the tree trembled so that one of the lights set fire to the green leaves. "Good gracious!" the young ladies exclaimed, and hastily put it out.

After this the tree tried to be calmer, for it was afraid of losing any of its splendor, but it felt dizzy from the glare. The doors were now thrown open, and a number of children rushed in, while the older people followed more slowly. For a moment the young ones stood still in admiration. But then their joy broke forth again, and they danced around the tree.

"What are they doing, and what will happen now?" the tree thought as one present after another was torn off. The tapers, too, began to burn down to the branches. And as they did so they were put out, and then the children received permission to plunder the tree. They fell upon it so that all the branches cracked. And if the top with the gold star had not been fastened to the ceiling, the whole tree would certainly have been thrown over.

The children danced about with their beautiful playthings, and no one looked at the tree, excepting the nursery-maid, who only looked to see whether a fig or an apple had been forgotten.

"A story! A story!" the children cried, and they dragged a little fat man up to the tree. He seated himself under it. "I shall only tell you one story," he said. "The one about Klumpe-Dumpe, who fell down the stairs but was still exalted and married the princess."

"Klumpe-Dumpe!" cried the children. But the fir tree was quiet and thought, "Shall I not have anything more to do with the evening's entertainment?"

67

The little man told the story, and the children clapped their hands, crying, "Go on! Go on!" The fir tree stood perfectly quiet and thoughtful. The birds in the forest had never told such stories as that of how Klumpe-Dumpe fell downstairs and yet married the princess. "Who can tell?" the fir tree thought. "Perhaps I may fall downstairs and marry a princess, too!" It rejoiced in the thought that the next night it would be adorned again with lights and playthings, fruits and gold.

"Tomorrow I shall not tremble," it thought. "I will enjoy my splendor thoroughly, and shall hear the story of Klumpe-Dumpe again." The tree stood in deep thought the whole night.

The next morning the servants came in. "Now it's going to begin again," the tree thought. But they carried it out of the room upstairs to the loft.

They put it in a dark corner where the daylight never reached. "What can this mean?" the tree thought. "What am I to do here, and what shall I hear, I wonder?" It leaned against the wall and thought and thought, and for that it had plenty of time. Days and nights passed without anyone coming up, and when at last someone did come, it was to bring up some large boxes to stand in the corner. The tree was quite hidden, and it seemed as if it were forgotten as well.

68

"It is now winter!" the tree thought. "The ground is hard and covered with snow, so that they cannot plant me. And so I am being taken care of here until spring. If it were but a little less dark and lonely here. Oh, how beautiful it was out in the forest when the snow lay on the ground, and the hare came running past, even when it jumped over me, though then I did not like it! It is dreadfully lonely up here!"

"Squeak! Squeak!" a little mouse said, coming forward cautiously. Then another came, and having sniffed at the tree, they crept between its branches.

"It is awfully cold here!" the little mice said. "Isn't it, you old fir tree?"

"I am not old!" the fir tree said. "There are many who are much older than I."

"Where have you been?" the mice asked. "What do you know?"

"I know the forest," the tree answered, "where the sun shines and the birds sing." And then it told them all about its youth. And the little mice, who had never heard anything like it before, listened with all their ears and said, "How happy you must have been!"

"Why happy?" the fir tree said, thinking over all it had been telling. "Yes, after all, those were happy times." But then it told them about Christmas Eve, when it was covered with cake and tapers.

"How well you talk!" the mice said. And the next night they came again with four others to listen to it. And the more it talked of the past, the more it thought, "Yes, those were happy times, and they may come again!"

After a time the little mice did not come any more. "It was quite pretty as they sat around me and listened," the tree sighed, "and now that is over, too. But I will not forget to enjoy it thoroughly when I am again taken out of here."

But when was that to happen? Well, one morning people came and took away the boxes. The tree, too, was dragged down the stairs.

The tree felt the fresh air and the sun, for it was now in the yard. It spread out its branches, but...oh, dear! They were quite dry and yellow. And there it lay among the rubbish. The gold star was still at its top, and it glittered in the sun.

A couple of the merry children who had danced round the fir tree on Christmas Eve were playing in the yard. One of them, seeing the star, ran and tore it off. "Look what was left on the ugly fir tree!" he said.

The tree looked at the flowers in the garden, then at itself, and wished it were back in its dark corner of the loft. It thought of its fresh youth, of the merry Christmas Eve, and of the little mice listening to its story.

"All is over now!" the poor tree said. "Oh, had I but enjoyed myself while I could!"

Then a servant came and chopped the tree into pieces for the kitchen fire. And as one piece after another was thrown in, it sighed. And at each sigh, the wood thought of a bright summer's day in the forest, or of a winter's night when the stars twinkled. It thought of Christmas Eve—and then the tree was gone.

The children played in the garden, and one of them wore the gold star that had been on the tree the happiest night of its life.

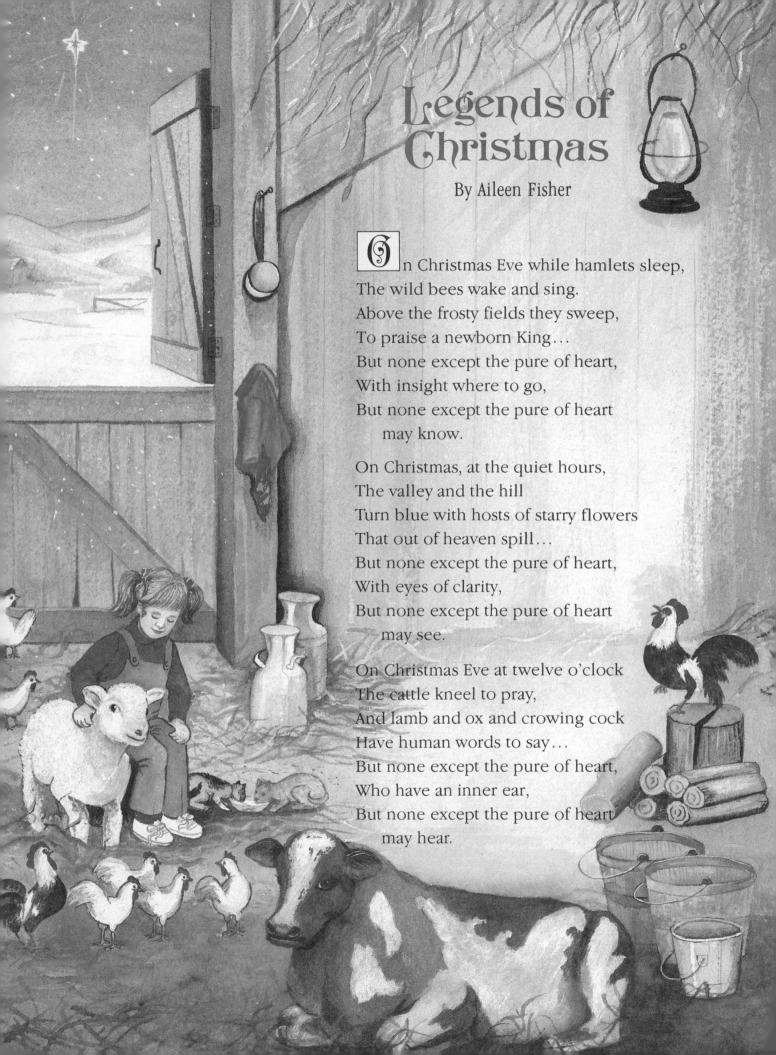

Legends of Christmas

By Aileen Fisher

On Christmas Eve while hamlets sleep,
The wild bees wake and sing.
Above the frosty fields they sweep,
To praise a newborn King…
But none except the pure of heart,
With insight where to go,
But none except the pure of heart
    may know.

On Christmas, at the quiet hours,
The valley and the hill
Turn blue with hosts of starry flowers
That out of heaven spill…
But none except the pure of heart,
With eyes of clarity,
But none except the pure of heart
    may see.

On Christmas Eve at twelve o'clock
The cattle kneel to pray,
And lamb and ox and crowing cock
Have human words to say…
But none except the pure of heart,
Who have an inner ear,
But none except the pure of heart
    may hear.

Hark!
The Herald Angels Sing

Words by Charles Wesley
Music by Felix Mendelssohn

Hark! the her-ald an-gels sing,_ "Glo-ry to the new-born King!

Peace on earth and mer-cy mild,_ God and sin-ners re-con-ciled."

Joy-ful, all ye na-tions rise,_ Join the tri-umph of the skies;

With th'an-gel-ic host pro-claim, "Christ is_born in Beth-le-hem!"

Hark! the her-ald an-gels sing, "Glo-ry_to the new-born King!"

The Christmas Story

Told by Jane Werner

This is Mary, a girl of Galilee.
She lived long years ago, but such a wonderful thing happened to her that we remember and love her still.

73

One day an angel appeared to Mary.
"You are blessed among women," the angel said. "For you shall have a son, whom you shall name Jesus. He shall be called the Son of God, and his kingdom shall never end."

"I am glad to serve the Lord," said Mary. "May it be as you have said."

Then the angel left her.

Mary married a good man from Nazareth. His name was Joseph, and he was a carpenter by trade.

When Joseph had to go from Nazareth up to Bethlehem in Judea, to pay his taxes in his father's town, Mary went with him. It was a long, weary journey for her.

When they reached Bethlehem at last, they found many travelers there before them. The streets were full of cheerful, jostling kinsmen.

The inns were crowded to the doors.
Though Joseph asked shelter only for his wife, every innkeeper turned them away.

At last one innkeeper, seeing Mary's weariness and need, showed them to a stable full of warm, sweet hay.

There Mary brought forth her son. And she wrapped him in
swaddling clothes and laid him in the manger, since there was no
room for them in the inn.

There were in that same country shepherds in the field, keeping watch over their flocks by night.

An angel of the Lord appeared to them in shining glory, and they were all afraid.

But the angel said to them:

"There is nothing to fear. I come to bring you news of a great joy that shall come to all people.

"For a child is born this day in Bethlehem—a Savior who is Christ the Lord.

"And this shall be a sign to you. You shall find the babe wrapped in swaddling clothes and lying in a manger."

Suddenly the sky was full of angels, praising God and saying, "Glory to God in the highest, and on Earth peace, good will toward men."

When the angels disappeared into heaven, the shepherds said to one another, "Let us go to Bethlehem and see this thing that the Lord has made known to us."

They hurried to the stable and found Mary and Joseph, and the babe lying in the manger. The shepherds knelt to honor the baby. Then they went back into town, singing praises to God for all they had seen and heard.

That night a bright star appeared in the East.

Three wise men followed the star until it stopped over the place where Jesus lay.

They entered the stable and saw the young child with Mary, his mother, and bowed down and worshipped him.

They opened their treasures and laid before him gifts: gold and frankincense and myrrh.

The child grew up to be strong in spirit and full of wisdom. And Mary knew the grace of God was upon him.

Silent Night

Words by Joseph Mohr
Music by Franz Grüber